This Ladybird Book belongs to:

_____

_____

_____

_____

This Ladybird retelling
by
Audrey Daly

Ladybird books are widely available, but in case of
difficulty may be ordered by post or telephone from:

Ladybird Books – Cash Sales Department
Littlegate Road Paignton Devon TQ3 3BE
Telephone 0803 554761

A catalogue record for this book is available
from the British Library

Published by Ladybird Books Ltd Loughborough Leicestershire UK
Ladybird Books Inc Auburn Maine 04210 USA

The Wizard
of Oz

illustrated
by
ANGUS McBRIDE

based on the story by L.Frank Baum

Once there was a little girl called Dorothy, who lived on the great Kansas prairie in America with her Aunt Em, her Uncle Henry and her dog Toto.

One day, when only Dorothy and Toto were at home, a whirlwind picked up the house and carried it away to a strange country.

"Where can I be?" Dorothy
wondered, as she looked around.

"You are in the eastern part of the
Land of Oz, where the Munchkins
live," said a little woman. "Thank you
so much for killing the Wicked Witch
of the East!"

Dorothy was very puzzled. She knew she had never killed anybody.

The little woman showed Dorothy two feet in silver slippers, sticking out from under the house. The Wicked Witch had been squashed!

"Those slippers are magic," said the little woman. "They belong to you now."

Dorothy put the slippers on. "My name is Dorothy," she explained politely. "Who are you?"

"I am the Good Witch of the North," replied the woman, "and my sister is the Good Witch of the South. Our enemies are the Wicked Witches of the East and West. Now, thanks to you, one of them is gone!"

Dorothy was pleased she had been helpful, but, more than anything, she wanted to go home. "How can I get back to Kansas?" she asked.

"Go and see the Wizard of Oz in the Emerald City," advised the Good Witch. "Just follow the Yellow Brick Road!"

After giving Dorothy a magic kiss to keep her safe, the Good Witch disappeared.

Dorothy put on a clean dress, and she and Toto set off.

Before long they met a scarecrow.
"Where are you going?" he asked.

When Dorothy told him, the
Scarecrow said, "Oh, please take me
with you. My head is full of straw, and
I want to ask the Wizard for a brain."

"All right," said Dorothy, lifting the
Scarecrow down from his pole.

So Dorothy, Toto and the Scarecrow walked on together. Soon they met a woodman working in the forest. He was made entirely of tin.

When Dorothy and the Scarecrow told him where they were going, the Woodman said, "I'd like to come with you, too, so I can ask the Wizard for a heart." He explained that the Wicked Witch of the East had turned him to tin and stolen his heart away.

Grrrrrrrr! A great lion jumped out at them. Dorothy smacked his nose. "Stop being such a bully!" she cried.

"I'm sorry," said the Lion. "I only act like that because everyone expects me to. But really I'm very frightened. Perhaps the Wizard could give me some courage."

They set off together, and soon they were all good friends.

At last they came to the Emerald City. A little green man came out to greet them.

"We've come to see the Wizard," said Dorothy, looking around in amazement. Everything was green – even the sky!

The little man gave each of them
a pair of green spectacles, and he
gave Dorothy a green dress to put
on. Then he led them to the palace.

"The Wizard will see you one at a
time," said the guard at the palace
door. "Dorothy can go first, because
she is wearing silver slippers."

Inside the palace, Dorothy was taken to the door of the throne room.

When she was finally allowed in, Dorothy saw an enormous bald head, with no body, arms or legs, on a large green throne.

"I am the great Wizard," said a squeaky voice. "Who are you?"

"I am Dorothy, and I'd like to go home to Kansas, please."

"Where did you get those silver slippers?" asked the Wizard.

Dorothy told him how the Wicked Witch of the East had died.

"Then, before you go back to Kansas, you must kill the Wicked Witch of the West as well!" squeaked the Wizard.

One by one Dorothy's friends went in to see the Wizard. Each time he appeared in a different shape, but his answer was always the same:

"You shall have your wish when the Wicked Witch is dead!"

"We will have to do as he says, or I will never get my courage!" said the Lion sadly.

"Nor I my brain!" said the Scarecrow.

"Nor I my heart!" added the Tin Woodman.

"And I will never get back to Kansas!" cried Dorothy. So they all set off to look for the Wicked Witch of the West.

Now the Wicked Witch of the West had heard that Dorothy and her friends were coming to kill her. She sent out fierce wolves to try to destroy them.

Dorothy was captured, but she couldn't be harmed, because the Good Witch's magic kiss protected her.

So the Wicked Witch forced Dorothy to scrub floors instead! This made Dorothy so angry that she threw the water all over the Witch.

"No!" shrieked the Witch. "Water will kill me!" And she melted away into a puddle.

The Wicked Witch was dead!

When Dorothy and her friends got
back to the Emerald City, they
couldn't find the Wizard anywhere
in the palace.

"What do you want?" a squeaky voice
asked from behind a screen.

"We've killed the Witch! And we want
you to keep your promises," said
Dorothy.

"I'll have to think about that! Come back tomorrow," the squeaky voice replied.

At that the Lion gave a huge roar. Toto was so surprised that he jumped up, and he knocked over the Wizard's screen.

Behind it, crouched down low, was a little old man. He looked very frightened indeed.

He wasn't a real wizard at all! But he was a kind man at heart, and he promised to try to help.

First he put some sawdust into the Scarecrow's head. "Now you've got a brain," he said.

Then he put a silk heart inside the Tin Woodman and gave the Lion some green medicine to give him courage. Everyone was so happy that the Wizard's magic worked after all.

"That wasn't magic," thought the little man to himself. "They were already clever, kind and brave. They just didn't know it!"

Only Dorothy's wish had not been granted. "Let's go and see if the Good Witch of the South can help," said the Scarecrow.

When the Good Witch heard Dorothy's story, she told her, "I can help you – but what will happen to the others when you have gone?"

"I have been asked to be ruler of the Emerald City," said the Scarecrow proudly.

"And the Winkies, who live nearby, have asked me to be *their* ruler," said the Tin Woodman.

"I'm going to be King of the Forest," said the Lion happily.

"But what about me?" asked Dorothy.

"You have the magic slippers, Dorothy," said the Good Witch. "All you have to do is tell them where you want to go."

"So I could have gone home that very first day!" cried Dorothy.

"But then you wouldn't have met *us!*" said the Scarecrow, the Tin Woodman and the Lion. Dorothy smiled at her friends and hugged them.

"Goodbye," she said. "I will never forget you." Then, picking up Toto, she cried, "Take me back to Kansas!"

The next thing Dorothy knew, she was in her Aunt Em's garden.

"Where have you come from?" asked her aunt in surprise.

"From the Land of Oz!" laughed Dorothy, kissing Aunt Em. "Oh, I'm *so* glad to be back."